DO NOT BRING YOUR DRAGON TO THE LAST DAY OF SCHOOL

WRITTEN BY Julie Gassman   ILLUSTRATED BY Andy Elkerton

CAPSTONE EDITIONS
a capstone imprint

On the last day of school, you smile when you wake.
It's been a great year, but you need a break.

You want the day to be **fantastic**,
so please avoid doing anything drastic . . .

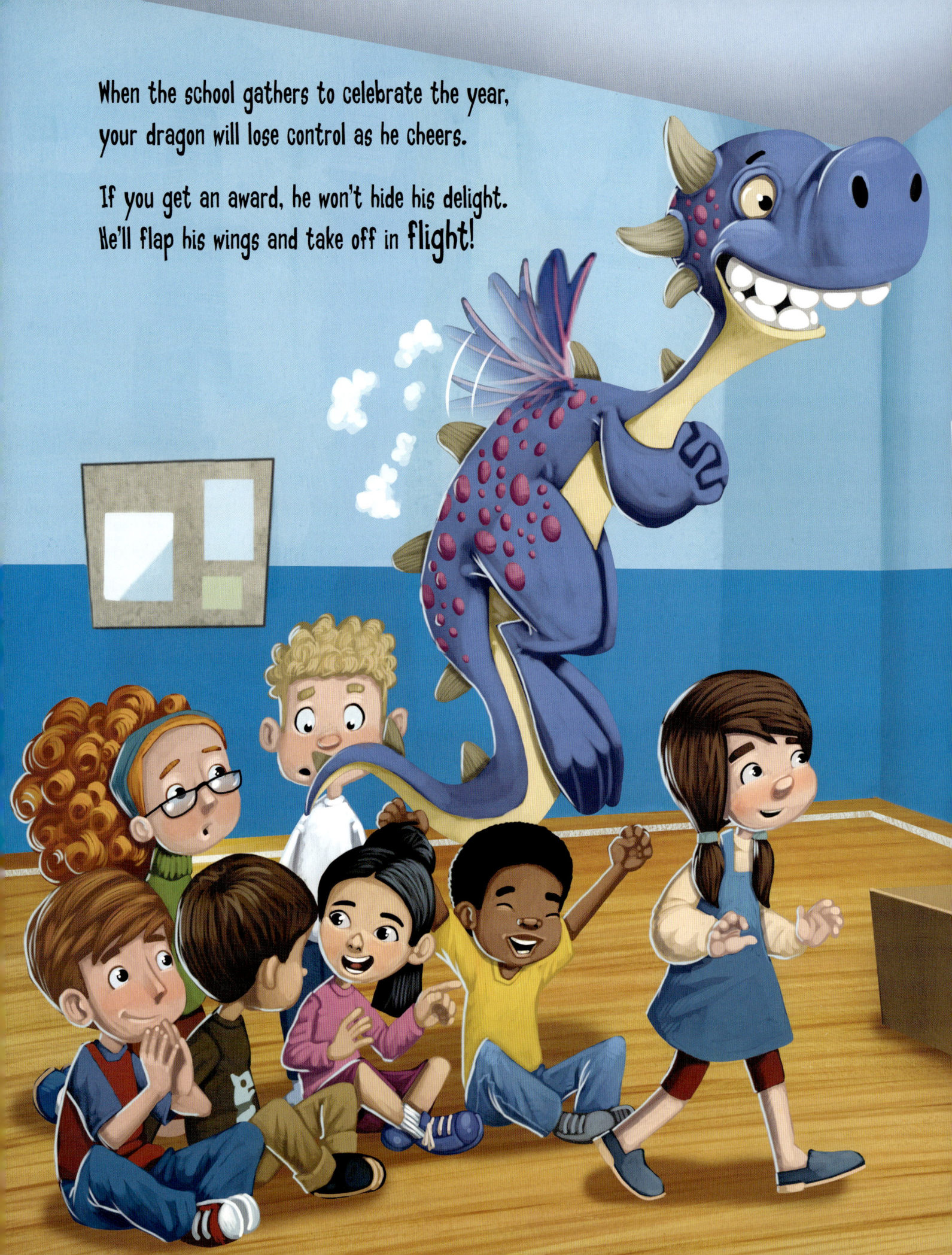

When the school gathers to celebrate the year,
your dragon will lose control as he cheers.

If you get an award, he won't hide his delight.
He'll flap his wings and take off in **flight!**

Back in the classroom, your desk is a mess.
It's a situation that you must address.

But all the dust will make dragon wheeze.
Then she'll let out an almighty sneeze!

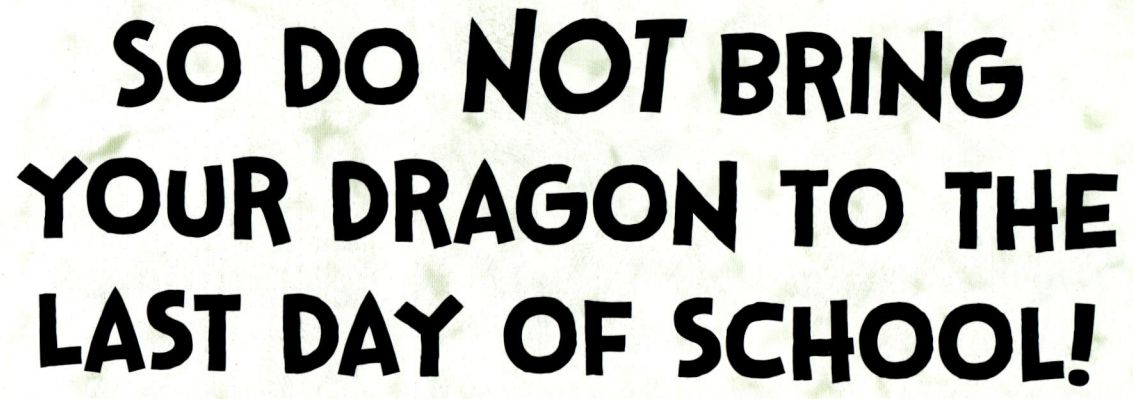

SO DO NOT BRING YOUR DRAGON TO THE LAST DAY OF SCHOOL!

It's a class picnic. You can't wait for **lunch**!
Then dragon sits down with a thunderous **crunch**!

He'll crowd your friends. He'll steal their dessert.
He'll even eat food that's been dropped in the dirt!

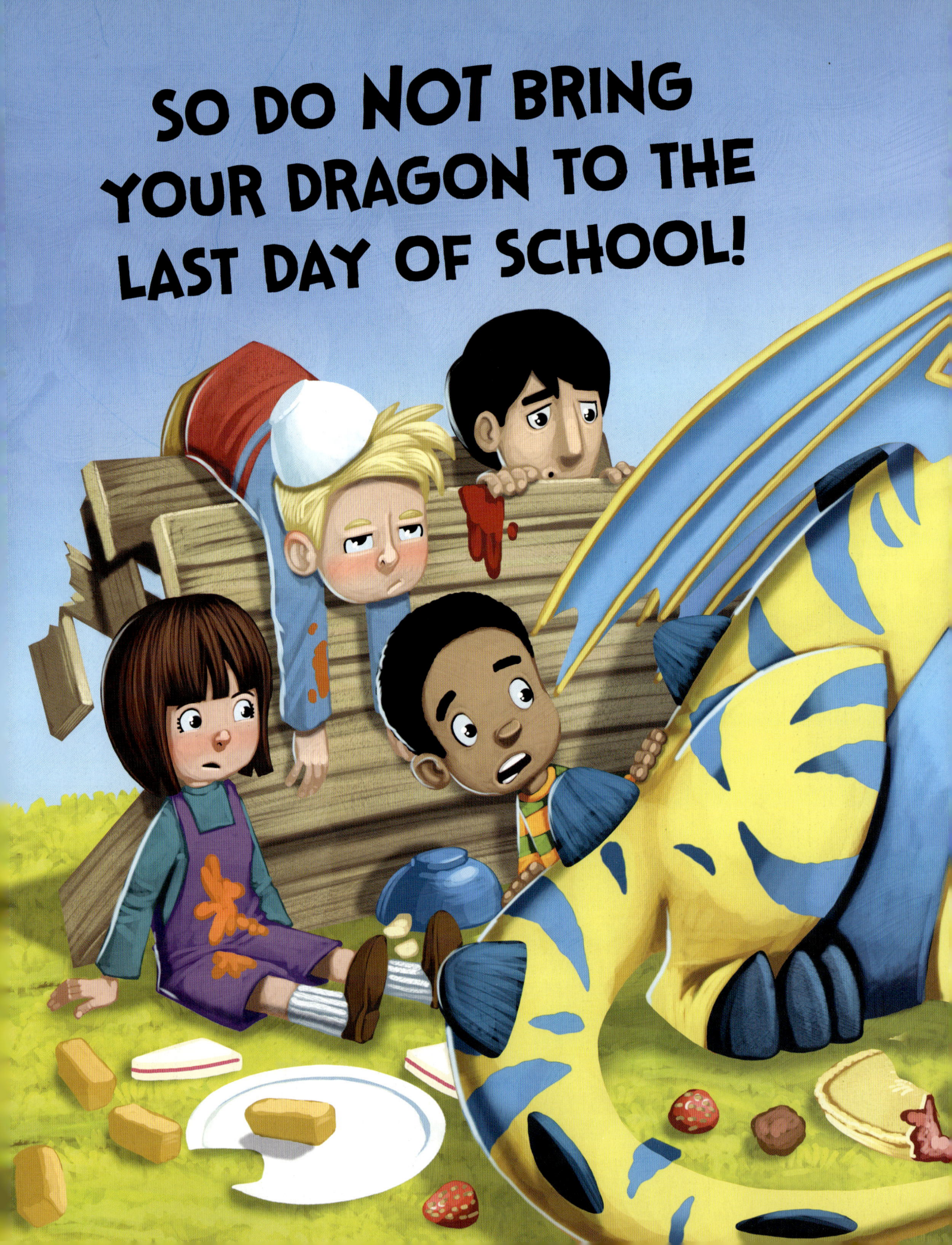

Dragon has no business playing field day games.
She tugs too hard and melts hoops with her flames.

And when it's time to compete in the three-legged race,
she'll trip the competition . . . what a **disgrace!**

I want to show him what makes school a **special place**.
The lunchroom, the playground, the makerspace!

And I want to show him how you make class so fun.
How smart you are—you've taught us **a ton!**

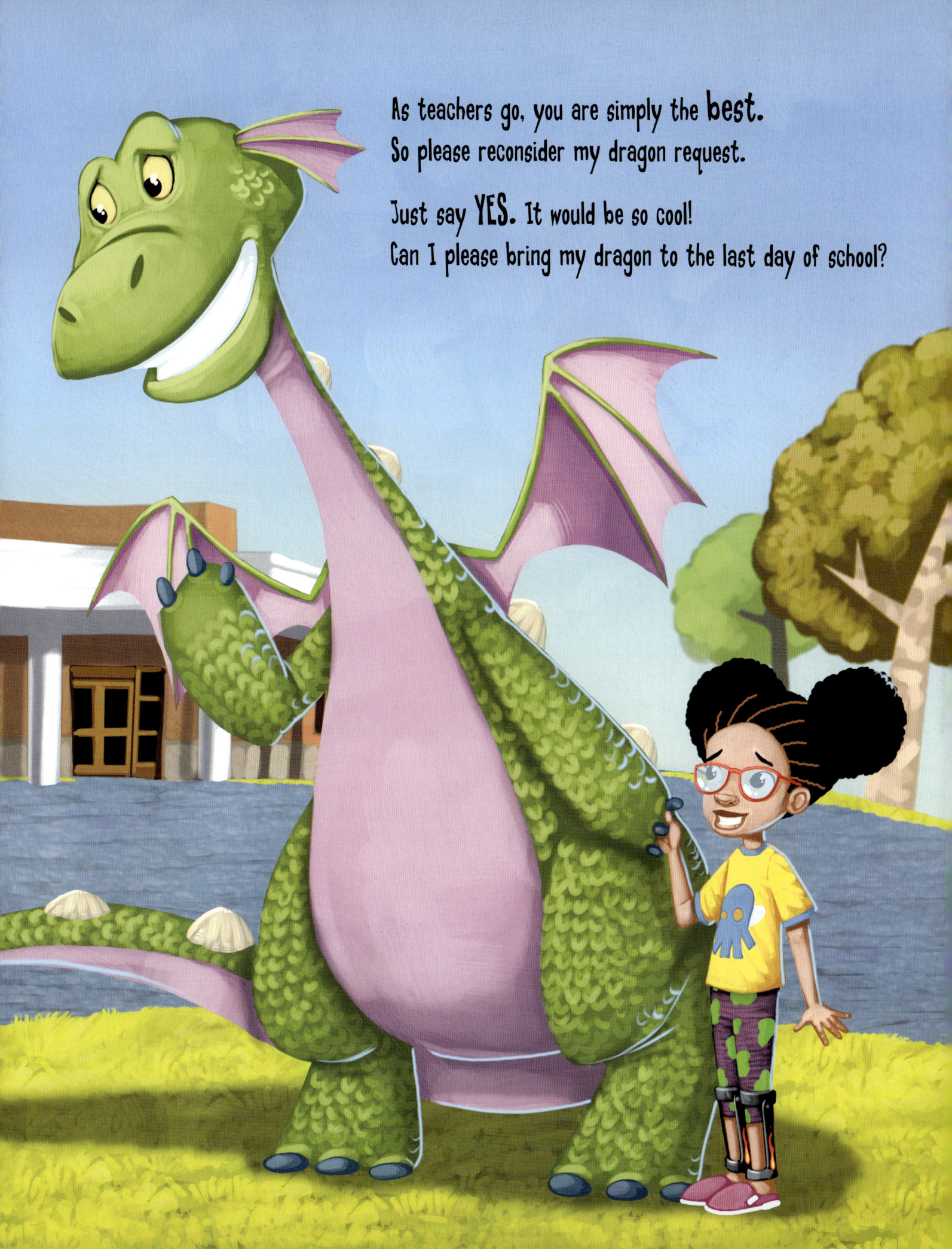

As teachers go, you are simply the **best**.
So please reconsider my dragon request.

Just say YES. It would be so cool!
Can I please bring my dragon to the last day of school?

It's been a fun year, but I want the class to myself.
I don't want to share the day with anyone else.

But perhaps he could come at the end of the day
and even join in the last game we play.

And if saying goodbye is hard, he'll put you at ease
with a big dragon smile and a sweet, loving **squeeze.**

A dragon hug is a wonderful tool . . .

ABOUT THE AUTHOR

The youngest in a family of nine children, Julie Gassman grew up in Howard, South Dakota. After college, she traded in small-town life for the world of magazine publishing in New York City. She now lives in southern Minnesota with her husband and their three children. On the last day of school, Julie and her dragon enjoy having water balloon fights and going out for ice cream.

ABOUT THE ILLUSTRATOR

After 14 years as a graphic designer, Andy decided to go back to his illustrative roots as a children's book illustrator. Since 2002 he has produced work for picture books, educational books, advertising, and toy design. Andy has worked for clients all over the world. He currently lives in a small tourist town on the west coast of Scotland with his wife and three children.

Do Not Bring Your Dragon to the Last Day of School
is published by Capstone Editions, an imprint of Capstone
1710 Roe Crest Drive, North Mankato, Minnesota 56003
www.capstonepub.com

Copyright © 2020 Capstone Editions, an imprint of Capstone
All rights reserved. No part of this publication may be reproduced
in whole or in part, or stored in a retrieval system, or transmitted in
any form or by any means, electronic, mechanical, photocopying,
recording, or otherwise, without written permission of the publisher.

Library of Congress Cataloging-in-Publication Data
Names: Gassman, Julie, author. | Elkerton, Andy, illustrator.
Title: Do not bring your dragon to the last day of school / written by
Julie Gassman ; illustrated by Andy Elkerton.
Description: [North Mankato, MN : Capstone Editions, 2020] |
Audience: Ages 4-7. | Audience: Grades K-1. |
Summary: A teacher points out many things that could go wrong
if she were to grant permission for a student to bring a dragon to
school on the last day.
Identifiers: LCCN 2019047399 (print) | LCCN 2019047400 (ebook) |
  ISBN 9781684460670 (hardcover) |
  ISBN 9781630793760 (paperback) |
  ISBN 9781684460687 (ebook pdf)
Subjects: CYAC: Stories in rhyme. | Dragons--Fiction. | Schools--
Fiction.
Classification: LCC PZ8.3.G199 Dq 2020 (print) | LCC PZ8.3.G199
(ebook) | DDC [E]--dc23
LC record available at https://lccn.loc.gov/2019047399
LC ebook record available at https://lccn.loc.gov/2019047400?

Designer: Nathan Gassman

Printed and bound in China. 6097